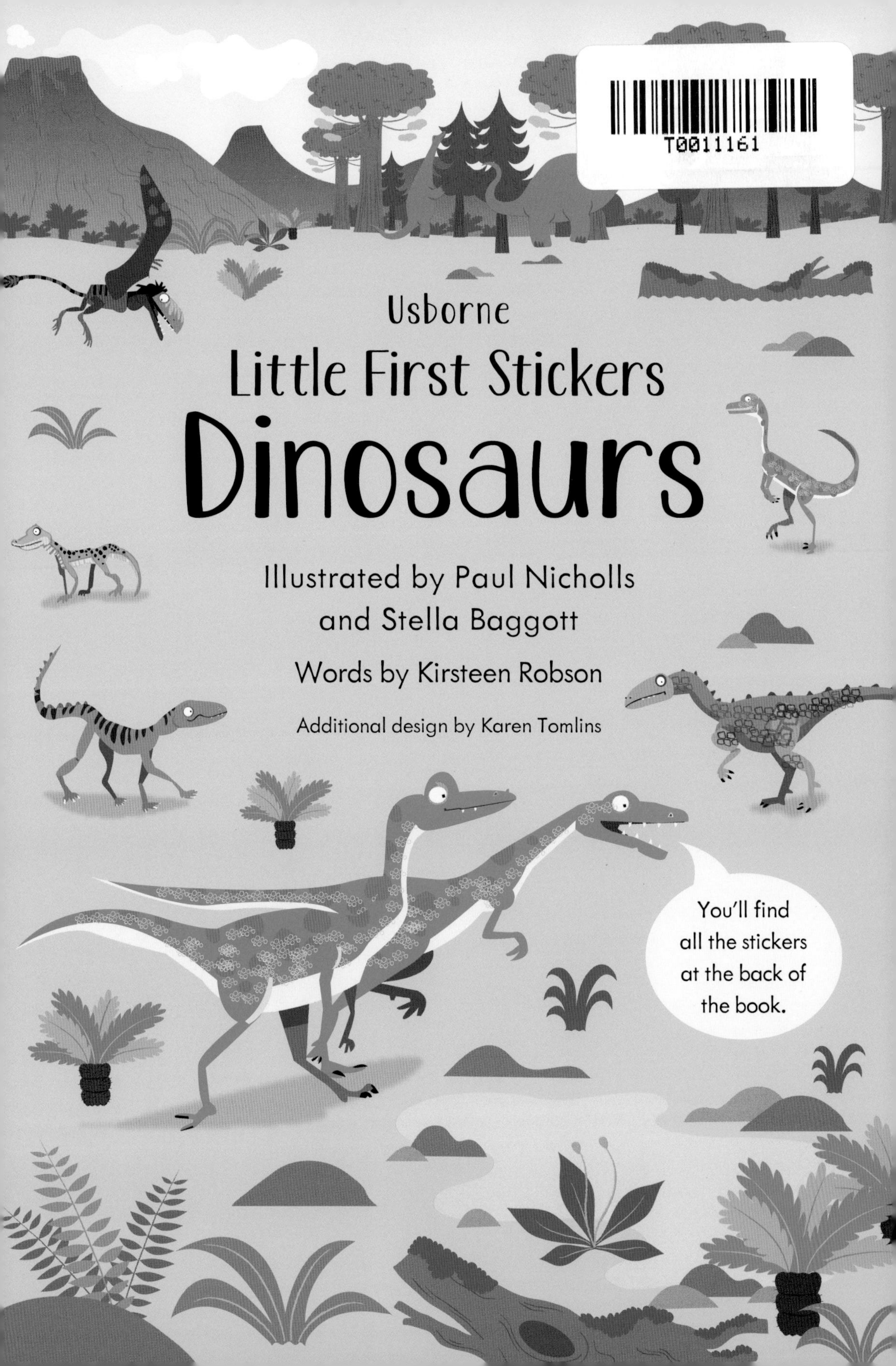

Usborne

Little First Stickers
Dinosaurs

Illustrated by Paul Nicholls
and Stella Baggott

Words by Kirsteen Robson

Additional design by Karen Tomlins

Eggs and nests

Cover the rocky ground with Oviraptor parents protecting their nests.

Show whose eggs have hatched out already.

Add more eggs
and trees.

Gentle giants

Stick on some long-necked leaf-munchers poking out between the trees.

Make two dinosaurs look like they're playing hide-and-seek!

On the hunt

Fill the page with fleeing dinosaurs who don't want to be this T. rex's lunch.

Add more spiky horsetails
in the undergrowth.

In the air

Stick on some winged reptiles
soaring high in the sky...

...and others swooping low
above the foamy waters.

Staying safe

Cover the page with Pinacosaurus parents defending their spiky offspring from a fierce T. rex.

Show some prehistoric reptiles flying by.

Triceratops trek

Arrange a herd of Triceratops plodding across the plain.

Stick on some plants that have not been trampled.

Under the sea

Fill the water with swimming reptiles of all shapes and sizes.

Add some prehistoric fish
darting between them.

By the river

Stand four Spinosauruses in the shallows, getting ready for a fishy feast.

Show three Spinosauruses squabbling on the sand.

Dinosaurs in danger

Cover the scorched landscape with dashing dinosaurs running for their lives.